MARGRET & H. A. REY'S
Curious George's
Dinosaur Discovery

Written by Catherine Hapka

Illustrated in the style of H. A. Rey by Vipah Interactive

Houghton Mifflin Harcourt

Boston New York

The text of this book is set in Adobe Garamond.
The illustrations are watercolor.

This special edition was printed for Kohl's Department Stores, Inc. (for distribution on behalf of
Kohl's Cares, LLC, its wholly owned subsidiary) by Houghton Mifflin Harcourt.

ISBN: 978-0-544-14905-2

Manufactured in China
SCP 10 9 8 7 6 5 4 3 2 1
4500400576

Kohl's
Style #: 978-0-544-14905-2
Factory #: 123386
Manufactured Date: 5/13

This is George.

He was a good little monkey and always very curious.

George loved to go places with his friend the man with the yellow hat. One of their favorite places to visit was the Dinosaur Museum.

"Today is a special day," George's friend said. "We are going to do something very interesting!"

George was curious. What could be more interesting than a trip to the Dinosaur Museum?

The man with the yellow hat led the way through the museum. George wanted to stop and look at the dinosaur bones. But his friend kept going, so George kept following.

Finally they walked right out the back door!

A van was waiting for them outside. "Climb in, George," said the man with the yellow hat.

George looked out the window as the van drove off. Where could they be going?

At last, the van reached a rocky quarry. Dozens of people were there. Some were digging with shovels. Others were using pickaxes or other kinds of tools.

"Surprise!" George's friend said. "We're going to help the museum scientists dig for dinosaur bones!"

George was curious. Were there really dinosaurs buried in the quarry? He ran over for a better look. "Hello," said a friendly scientist. "Are you here to help with the dig?"

George watched the scientist work. She dug up some dirt and put it into her sifting pan.

It took a long time to sift it. And in the end — no dinosaur bones!

"Oh, well," she said. "Time to try again!"

But the next pan was empty, too. So was the next one. And the one after that.

George yawned. So far digging for dinosaurs was not as exciting as he'd expected.

George was curious. Could he help to find dinosaur bones?

He found a spare shovel lying nearby. He dug and dug.
But he didn't find any dinosaurs.

When he climbed out of his hole, George spotted another scientist. He was dusting something with a small brush.

"Oh, well," the scientist said. "It's not a bone. Just a rock."

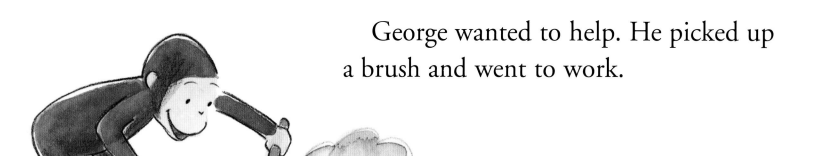

George wanted to help. He picked up
a brush and went to work.

But it turns out that monkeys are
not very good at dusting!

As he hurried away from the cloud of dust, George bumped into a wheelbarrow. Maybe there were dinosaur bones in it!

He climbed up to look inside. But the wheelbarrow was awfully tippy . . .

CRASH!

George, the wheelbarrow, and a whole lot of dirt went flying.
"Hey!" someone cried. "What's that monkey doing?"

George scampered away, straight up the cliff. Monkeys are good at climbing, so George kept going — higher and higher.

When he got to the top, he accidentally knocked a stone over the edge.

That stone hit another stone . . .

which hit another stone . . .

and another . . .

Oh, no! It was a rockslide!

19

The man with the yellow hat called for George to come down. George wanted to climb down, but he was afraid the scientists would be angry with him.

But the scientists didn't look angry.

"Look!" one cried, pointing. "Look what that monkey just uncovered!"

20

George could hardly believe what he saw. Dinosaur bones!

After that, the dinosaur dig was even more fun. George helped the scientists dig . . .

and sift . . .

and dust . . .

and take photographs of
the bones he had found.

And the next time he and the man with the yellow hat visited the Dinosaur Museum, George got to see HIS dinosaur on display!